Ladybird books are widely available, but in case of
difficulty may be ordered by post or telephone from:

Ladybird Books – Cash Sales Department
Littlegate Road Paignton Devon TQ3 3BE
Telephone 0803 554761

A catalogue record for this book is available
from the British Library

Published by Ladybird Books Ltd Loughborough Leicestershire UK
Ladybird Books Inc Auburn Maine 04210 USA

THE
TALE OF
JEMIMA
PUDDLE-DUCK™

Based on the original and authorized story
by Beatrix Potter
Ladybird Books in association with Frederick Warne

Jemima Puddle-duck was annoyed because the farmer's wife would not let her hatch her own eggs.

Jemima's sister-in-law, Mrs Rebeccah Puddle-duck, was perfectly willing to leave the hatching to someone else.

"I have not the patience to sit on a nest for twenty-eight days, and no more have you, Jemima. You would let them go cold, you know you would!" she said.

"I wish to hatch my own eggs. I will hatch them all by myself!" quacked Jemima.

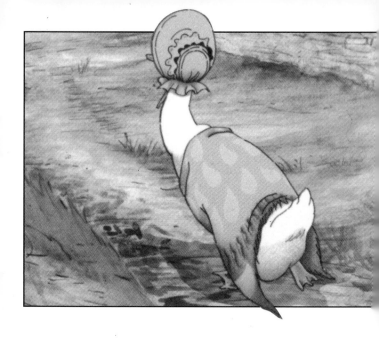

Jemima decided to make a nest right away from the farm. She set off along the cart-road that leads over the hill. She was wearing a shawl and a poke bonnet.

When she reached the top of the hill, she saw a wood in the distance. She thought that it looked a safe, quiet spot.

Jemima Puddle-duck was not much in the habit of flying. She ran downhill flapping her shawl, and then she jumped into the air. She flew beautifully when she got a good start.

Jemima saw an open place in the middle of the wood. She landed rather heavily and began to waddle about in search of a convenient dry nesting-place. She rather liked the look of a tree-stump amongst some tall fox-gloves. But – seated upon the stump was an elegantly dressed gentleman reading a newspaper.

The gentleman raised his eyes above his newspaper.

"Madam, have you lost your way?" he asked.

Jemima explained that she had not lost her way, but that she was trying to find a convenient dry nesting-place.

"Ah! Is that so? Indeed!" said the gentleman with sandy whiskers, looking curiously at Jemima. He folded up his newspaper and put it in his coat-tail pocket.

"I have a sackful of feathers in my wood-shed. No, my dear madam, you will be in nobody's way. You may sit there as long as you like," he told Jemima.

He led the way to a dismal-looking house amongst the fox-gloves.

"This is my summer residence. You would not find my earth – my winter house – so convenient," said the hospitable gentleman. He opened the door and showed Jemima in.

Jemima Puddle-duck was rather surprised to find such a vast quantity of feathers. But it was very comfortable, and she made a nest without any trouble at all.

When Jemima came out, the sandy-whiskered gentleman was sitting on a log reading the newspaper – at least he had it spread out, but he was looking over the top of it.

He was so polite that he seemed almost sorry to let Jemima go home for the night. He promised to take great care of her nest until she came back the next day.

Jemima Puddle-duck came every afternoon. She laid nine eggs. They were greeny white and very large.

The foxy gentleman admired them immensely. He used to turn them over and count them when Jemima was not there.

At last Jemima told him that she intended to begin to sit the next day.

"I will bring a bag of corn with me so that I need never leave my nest until the eggs are hatched. They might catch cold," said the conscientious Jemima.

"Madam," said the foxy gentleman, "I beg you not to trouble yourself with a bag. I will provide oats. But before you commence your tedious sitting, I intend to give you a treat. Let us have a dinner party all to ourselves!"

He asked Jemima to bring some herbs from the farm-garden to make a savoury omelette. Sage and thyme, and mint and two onions, and some parsley.

"I will provide lard for the stuff – lard for the omelette," he added.

Jemima Puddle-duck was a simpleton. Not even the mention of sage and onions made her suspicious. She went round the farm-garden, nibbling off snippets of all the different sorts of herbs that are used for stuffing roast duck.

Jemima waddled into the kitchen and got two onions out of a basket. The collie-dog Kep met her coming out.

"What are you doing with those onions? Where do you go by yourself every afternoon?" he asked.

Jemima told Kep the whole story. He grinned when she described the polite gentleman with sandy whiskers.

Kep asked
several questions
about the wood and about
the exact position of the house and
shed. Then he went out to look for
two fox-hound puppies.

Jemima Puddle-duck went up the cart-road, rather burdened with bunches of herbs and two onions in a bag.

When she reached the shed, the bushy-tailed gentleman was sitting on a log, glancing uneasily round the wood.

"Come into the house as soon as you have looked at your eggs. Give me the herbs for the omelette. Be sharp!" he said abruptly.

Jemima felt surprised and uncomfortable.

While she was inside she heard the pattering of feet round the back of the shed.

Someone with a black nose sniffed at the bottom of the door and then locked it. Jemima became much alarmed.

A moment afterwards there were the most awful barking, baying, growls and howls, squealing and groans. And nothing more was ever seen of that foxy-whiskered gentleman.

Presently Kep opened the door of the shed and let out Jemima Puddle-duck.

Unfortunately the puppies rushed in
and gobbled up all the eggs before
Kep could stop them. He had a bite
on his ear and both the puppies were
limping.

Jemima Puddle-duck was escorted home in tears on account of those eggs.

She laid some more in June and she was permitted to keep them herself, but only four of them hatched.

Jemima Puddle-duck said that it was because of her nerves, but she had always been a bad sitter.